The Story of
WINNIE THE POOH AND TIGGER

gb
GOLDEN PRESS
Western Publishing Company, Inc.
Racine, Wisconsin

1978 Special Edition

GOLDEN PRESS® is a re[gistered trademark of We]stern Publishing Company, Inc.

Christopher Robin was a little boy who had a teddy
bear named Winnie the Pooh. Sometimes he called him
Pooh Bear. Sometimes, — just Pooh.

1

Pooh lived in a magic forest — the Hundred Acre Wood — under the name of "Sanders." But today Pooh was not home. He was out in the woods, visiting his friends.

It was such a windy day that Pooh had been wishing his friends a Happy Windsday. Finally the weather got a bit *too* windy, even for Pooh. He decided to go home.

Now Pooh was always hungry, and the thing he liked best to eat was honey. So as soon as he got in the house, Pooh took down one of his honey pots—he had a great many—and began to eat.

While Pooh was eating his dinner, the windy day turned into a windy night. Pooh decided to go to bed. He put on his nightcap, climbed in, and pulled up the covers.

But Pooh could not sleep. He kept hearing all sorts of squeaky, windy, creaky noises. Then he heard a different kind of noise entirely. It sounded like BROWWWWER!

Pooh jumped out of bed, lighted his candle, and looked around. Then he decided to be very brave — or very silly. He invited the new noise into his house. "Hello out there!" he said, hoping nobody would answer.

7

But somebody did answer. "Hello! I'm Tigger," said a voice. And into the room—bounding and bouncing as if he were made of rubber—came a large orangey animal.

"Whew! You scared me!" said Pooh.

"Of course I did. Everyone's scared of Tiggers," said Tigger.

"And who are you?" he said to Pooh.
"I'm Pooh," said Pooh.
"What's a Pooh?" said Tigger.
"You are sitting on one," said Pooh.

"Glad to meet you," said Tigger. I'm new around here. Name's spelled T...I...G...G...E...R, that's Tigger."

While he was looking around Pooh's house, Tigger found a mirror. "Well! Who is that with the beady eyes and the striped pajamas?" he asked Pooh.

Pooh came over to the mirror. "Looks like just another Tigger," he said.

"Can't be," said Tigger. "I'm the only Tigger there is." (Which was quite true, of course.)

14

"Tell you what," he said to Pooh. "Watch me scare the stripes off him!" With that, he gave out a great big ROAAARRRR.

The Tigger in the mirror ROAAARRRRed right back at him!

Tigger bounced back from the mirror in a great hurry.

In fact, he was so scared that he ran and hid under
Pooh's bed. All Pooh could see of him was his tail.

"Is he gone?" asked Tigger.
"All but the tail," said Pooh.

18

With that, Tigger came out from under the bed and
found that he was all alone with Pooh. He gave a big sigh
of relief. "I'm hungry," he said, rubbing his tummy.

Right then Pooh thought of his lovely pots of honey. There were only twelve of them—or was it eleven? Slowly he took down two—one for Tigger and one for himself. "What would you like to eat?" he asked politely. "Some...honey?"

"Yeeech!" said Tigger. "That icky, sticky stuff! It's only fit for heffalumps and woozles." He jumped around as if he had honey all over him.

"You mean elephants and weasels?" asked Pooh.

"That's what I said—heffalumps and woozles," said Tigger. "If you don't have anything else to eat, I'd better be bouncing along." He said goodbye to Pooh and went out the door.

As soon as he left, Pooh sat down and ate one of the pots of honey. Then — because there really was no point in putting the other one back on the shelf — he ate that too. Tiggers were wonderful — and they didn't like honey.

23